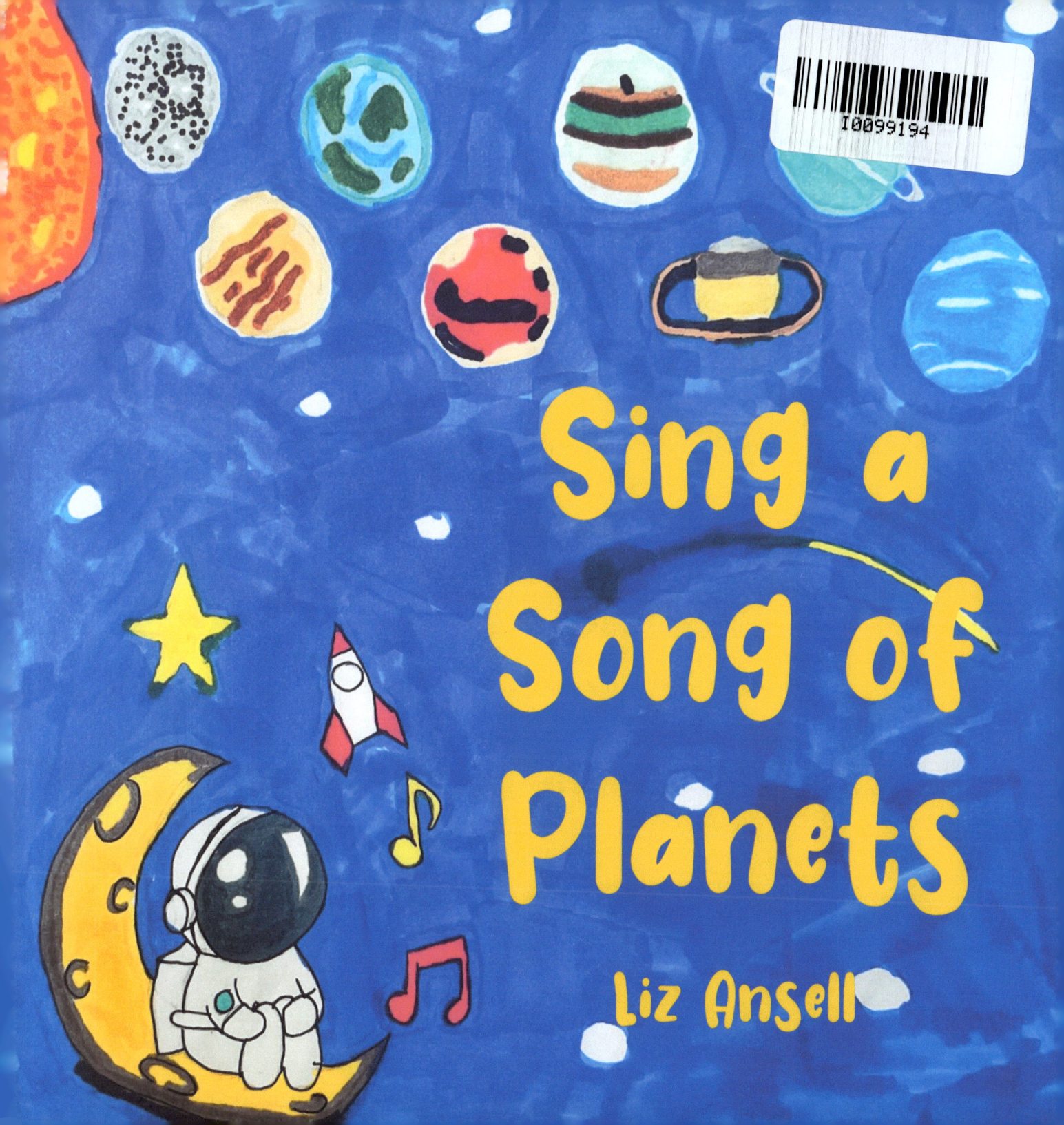

# Sing a Song of Planets

Liz Ansell

First published 2024
by Rowanvale Books Ltd
The Gate
Keppoch Street
Roath
Cardiff
CF24 3JW
www.rowanvalebooks.com
Library Cataloguing in Publication Data.
A catalogue record for this book is available from the British Library.

# A big thank you...

...to the wonderful children of the following schools, in the town of Weston-super-Mare:

Milton Park Primary

Oldmixon Primary

St Martin's C of E Primary

Worle Village Primary

Who have provided both the illustrations and singing for this book.

# Contents

Olivia Year 1
at Oldmixon primary

Bang

Bar

Bang

Bang

Borg

Bang

Bang

# There Are Three Firecrackers

**(Sing to the tune of 'She'll Be Coming 'Round the Mountain')**

There are three firecrackers in the street.
BANG, BANG, BANG!
There are three firecrackers in the street.
BANG, BANG, BANG!
There are three firecrackers,
There are three firecrackers,
There are three firecrackers in the street.
BANG, BANG, BANG!

There are two firecrackers in the street.
BANG, BANG!
There are two firecrackers in the street.
BANG, BANG!
There are two firecrackers,
There are two firecrackers,
There are two firecrackers in the street.
BANG, BANG!

There is one firecracker in the street.
BANG!
There is one firecracker in the street.
BANG!
There is one firecracker,
There is one firecracker,
There is one firecracker in the street.
BANG!

There are no firecrackers, only smoke.
PUFF, PUFF!
There are no firecrackers, only smoke.
PUFF, PUFF!
There are no firecrackers,
There are no firecrackers,
There are no firecrackers,
only smoke.
PUFF, PUFF!

# Pancake Poem

Let's make some pancakes using eggs, milk and flour,

Then once they're cooked, we can make a pancake tower

Of one, two, three, four,

Five, six or maybe more,

Then we'll add some sugar and lemon too,

Yummy pancakes for me and you.

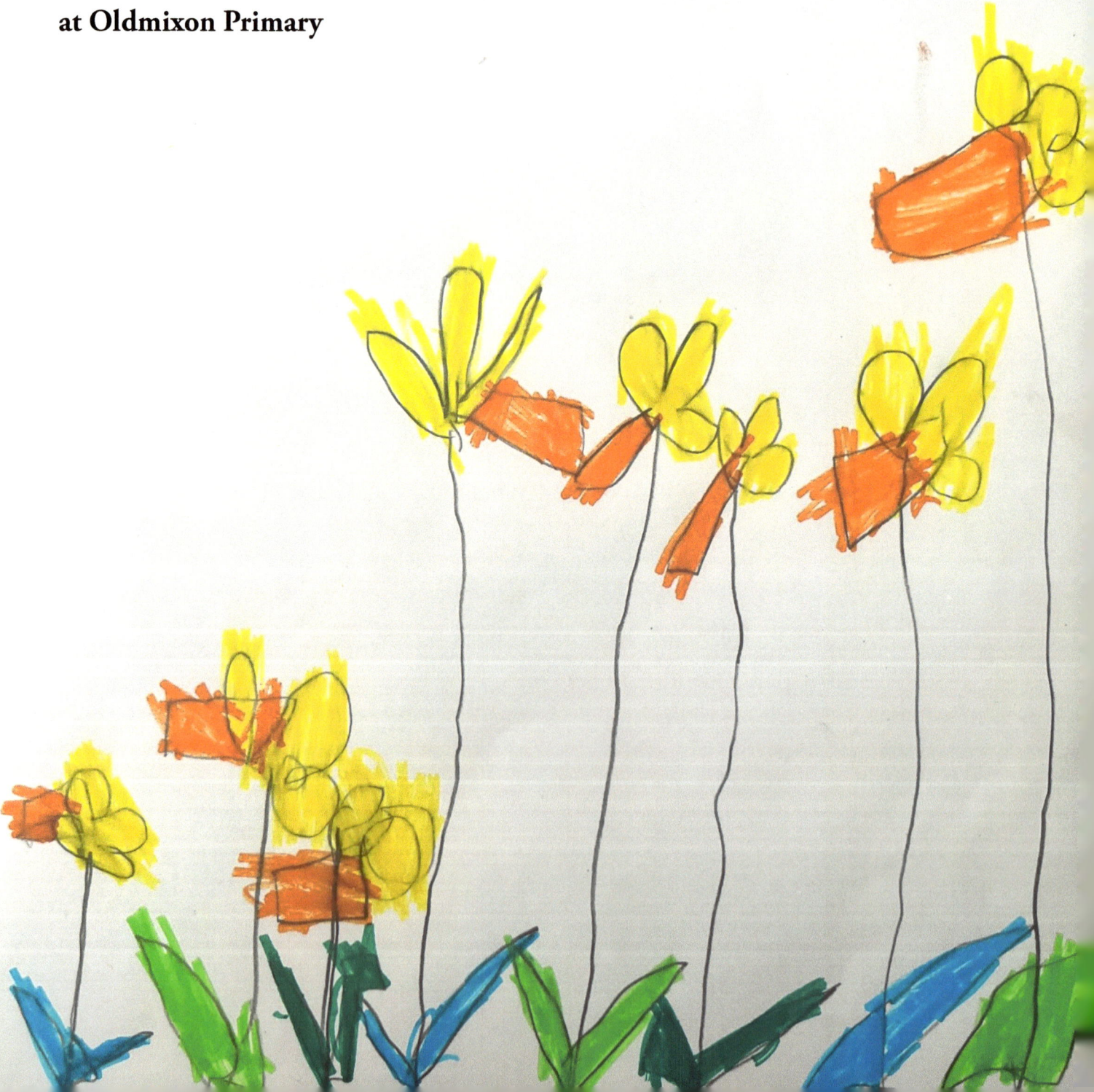

# Happy Saint David's Day

### (Sing to the tune of 'Pop Goes the Weasel')

Dydd Gŵyl Dewi Hapus,

This is what we say.

Dydd Gŵyl Dewi Hapus,

On Saint David's Day.

The first of March is a special day,

A time for celebration.

So pin on a leek or a daffodil,

And join in the jubilation.

# A Bunch of Flowers

**(Sing to the tune of 'This Old Man')**

A bunch of flowers, I give to you,
To say thank you for all you do.
Of red and yellow, pink, blue and white,
Tied in a bow all pretty and bright.

Sienna Year 1
at St Martins C of E Primary

# My Dad's Special

**(Sing to the tune of 'Little Peter Rabbit')**

My dad's special from his head down to his toes,

My dad's special from his head down to his toes,

My dad's special from his head down to his toes,

Every day my love for him just grows and grows and grows.

Crazy hair and bristly whiskers,

Crazy hair and bristly whiskers,

Crazy hair and bristly whiskers,

Every day my love for him just grows and grows and grows.

Jasmine Year 4
at Milton Park Primary

# Build a Bonfire

**(Sing to the tune of 'Oh My Darling, Clementine')**

Build a bonfire, build a bonfire.
Can you build it nice and high?
Build a bonfire, build a bonfire.
Can you build it to the sky?

Put some sticks on, put some sticks on.
Can you build it nice and high?
Put some sticks on, put some sticks on.
Can you build it to the sky?

Put some leaves on, put some leaves on.
Can you build it nice and high?
Put some leaves on, put some leaves on.
Can you build it to the sky?

Put the Guy on, put the Guy on.
Can you put him at the top?
Put the Guy on, put the Guy on,
And when you've finished, you can stop!

Ella Year 3
at Martins C of E Primary

Help!!!

Hotel

# Oh, Father Christmas IS Stuck Down My Chimney!

**(Sing to the tune of 'There's a Worm at the Bottom of My Garden')**

Oh, Father Christmas is stuck down my chimney,

And I don't think he'll ever get out.

Oh, Father Christmas is stuck down my chimney,

And all he can do is shout!

And wriggle like this and wriggle like that,

He'll never get out, his tummy's too fat.

Oh, Father Christmas is stuck down my chimney,

And I don't think he'll ever get out.

GOOD FOOD

Leo Year 4
at Milton Park Primary

MR MAN

BAD FOOD

TAKIS

ARES

OREO

MONSTER

# What Can You Eat?

**(Sing to the tune of 'Skip to My Lou')**

What can you eat every day?
What can you eat every day?
What can you eat every day?
To keep you nice and healthy.

Apples, pears and melon, too,
Apples, pears and melon, too,
Apples, pears and melon, too,
To keep you nice and healthy.

What can you eat, once in a while?
What can you eat, once in a while?
What can you eat, once in a while?
A treat that is sweet or savoury.

Biscuits, crisps and pizza, too,
Biscuits, crisps and pizza, too,
Biscuits, crisps and pizza, too,
A treat that is sweet or savoury.

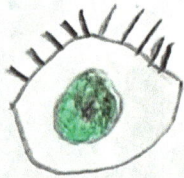

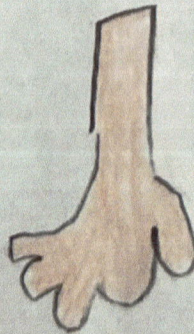

Antonina Year 1
at St Martins C of E Primary

# I Can See

**(Sing to the tune of 'Head, Shoulders, Knees and Toes')**

I can see and hear and smell,

Hear and smell.

And I can taste and touch as well,

Touch as well.

With my eyes and ears and mouth and nose,

And not forgetting my fingers and toes.

Hazel Year R
at Worle Village Primary

# Up From the Earth (Poem)

Up from the earth came a little green shoot,
Down in the earth goes its great big root.
The shoot grows up and the root grows down,
And that's how plants grow all around.

A Year 4 collaboration
at Milton Park Primary

# Bubbles, Bubbles Everywhere

**(Sing to the tune of 'Twinkle, Twinkle Little Star')**

Bubbles, bubbles everywhere,
Bubbles floating in the air.
Up above the world so high,
Rainbow colours in the sky.
Now my bubbles float away,
How I wish that they would stay!

Sun

Jupiter

Moon

Mercury

Saturn

Venus

Earth

Uranus

Mars

Neptune

Pluto

Phoebe year 4
at Worle Village primary

# Sing a Song of Planets!

**(Sing to the tune of 'Sing a Song of Sixpence')**

Sing a song of planets, up in space so high.
Can you name their order? Let's see if you can try.

Let's start with planet Mercury, 'cause it is number one,
Also, it's the smallest and closest to the sun.

Sing a song of planets, now Venus takes its place.
Shining oh so brightly, up in outer space.

The next is planet Earth, the place that we all tread.
Then after us is planet Mars, which we all know is red.

Sing a song of planets, now Jupiter takes a turn.
It's really quite enormous, with lots of gas to burn.

And then there's planet Saturn, with rings of ice and rock.
And finally, there's Uranus, and Neptune's where we stop!

Bianka Year 1
at Worle Village primary

# Comet Bright

**(Sing to the tune of 'Jingle Bells')**

Shooting through the sky, the comet makes its way.
Travelling all the while, all through the night and day.
Orbiting the sun, its gasses start to warm,
Glowing very bright, a tail begins to form.

Comet bright, comet bright,
Shooting through the sky,
Oh, what fun you are to watch,
I love to see you fly – Hey!

Comet bright, comet bright,
Shooting through the sky,
Oh, what fun you are to watch,
I love to see you fly – Hey!

Kaysie Year 4
at Milton Park primary

# Stars Are Burning

**(Sing to the tune of 'London's Burning')**

Stars are burning, stars are burning,

See their light, see their light,

Fire, fire, fire, fire.

Balls of gasses, balls of gasses,

Burning bright, burning bright.

# Author Profile

Liz Ansell presently resides in the seaside town of Weston-super-Mare with husband, James; mother, Marlene; and two children, Charlotte and Cameron. She is proud to share with you her collection of original songs and poems, which have been beautifully illustrated by the children of several primary schools in the local area.

She has worked with children for more than thirty years in a variety of settings. Most of this time was spent working in a local primary school where, once her talents were discovered, she was asked to write stories, songs and poems for the children to enjoy, as well as plays for them to perform. More recently, she has become a children's storyteller and has acted out stories to children of all ages, including babies. The stories she tells are often ones she has written, and they are always accompanied by songs/rhymes, many of which are featured in this book. At home, she can often be found in her kitchen, singing and dancing around, much to the embarrassment of her children!

# What did you think of SING A SONG OF PLANETS?

A big thank you for purchasing this book. It means a lot that you chose this book specifically from such a wide range on offer. I do hope you enjoyed it.

Book reviews are incredibly important for an author. All feedback helps them improve their writing for future projects and for developing this edition. If you are able to spare a few minutes to post a review on Amazon, that would be much appreciated.

## Publisher Information

rowanvale books

Rowanvale Books provides publishing services to independent authors, writers and poets all over the globe. We deliver a personal, honest and efficient service that allows authors to see their work published, while remaining in control of the process and retaining their creativity. By making publishing services available to authors in a cost-effective and ethical way, we at Rowanvale Books hope to ensure that the local, national and international community benefits from a steady stream of good quality literature.

For more information about us, our authors or our publications, please get in touch.
www.rowanvalebooks.com
info@rowanvalebooks.com

www.ingramcontent.com/pod-product-compliance
Lightning Source LLC
Chambersburg PA
CBHW041551040426
42447CB00002B/134